With love to my husband, Mike, and our
wonderful children, Susie and Jonathan — B. W.

For my husband, Darius, and the wonderful boys,
Milo, Reuben, Silas and Jack — R. O.

# Outdoor Opposites

Written by Brenda Williams • Illustrated by Rachel Oldfield

Sung by The Flannery Brothers

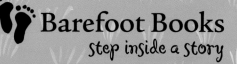

Barefoot Books
step inside a story

I can stand up,

or I can
sit down.

I can smile,

or I can frown.

I can run,

or I can walk.

I can listen,

or I can...

talk!

Low!

I am doing opposites.

Fast!

Slow!

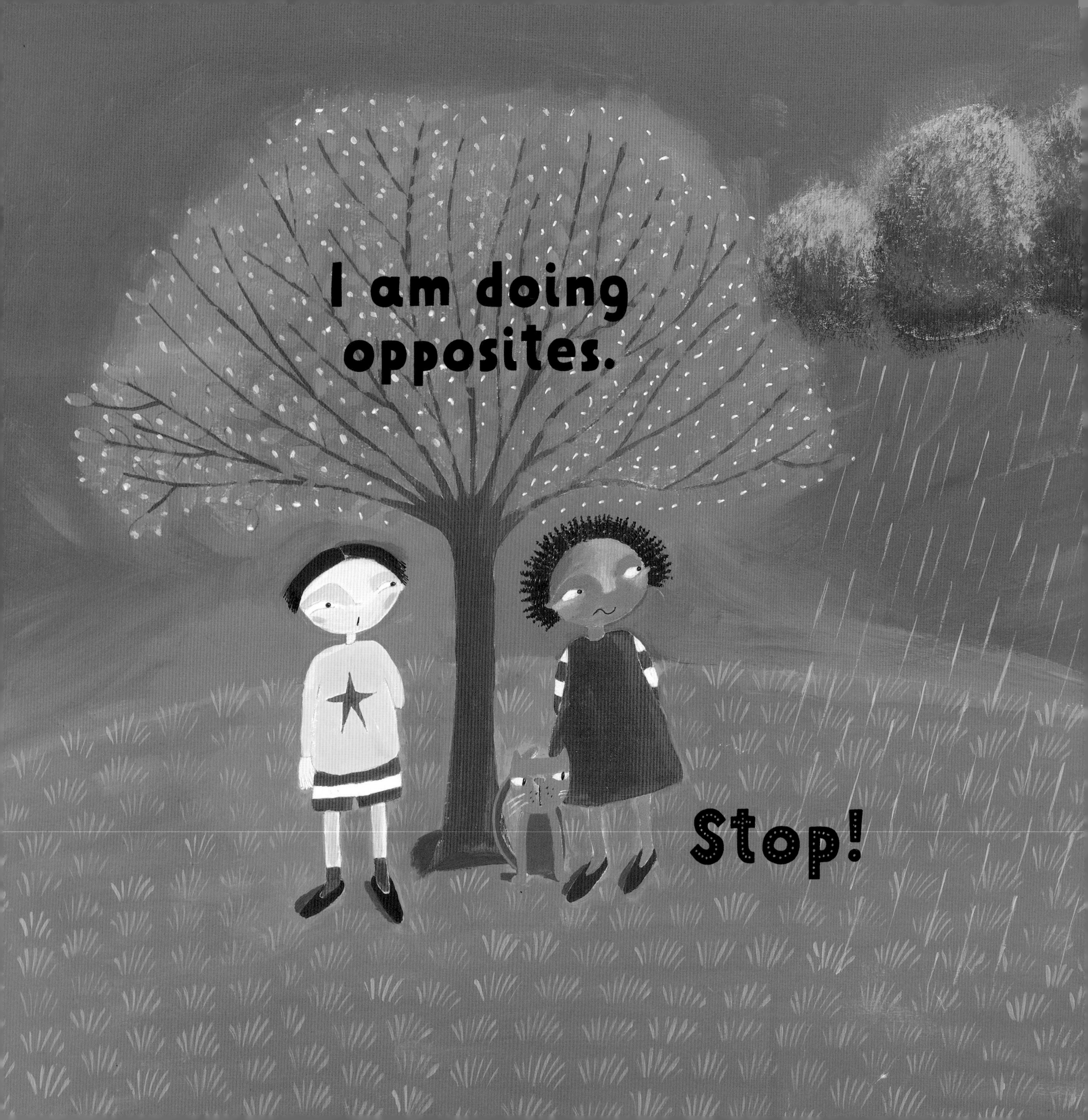

I am doing opposites.

Stop!

I can whisper,

or I can...

or I can jump OUT.

I can
taste good
things,

or I can
taste bad.

I can be happy,

or I can be sad.

Show!

I am doing opposites.

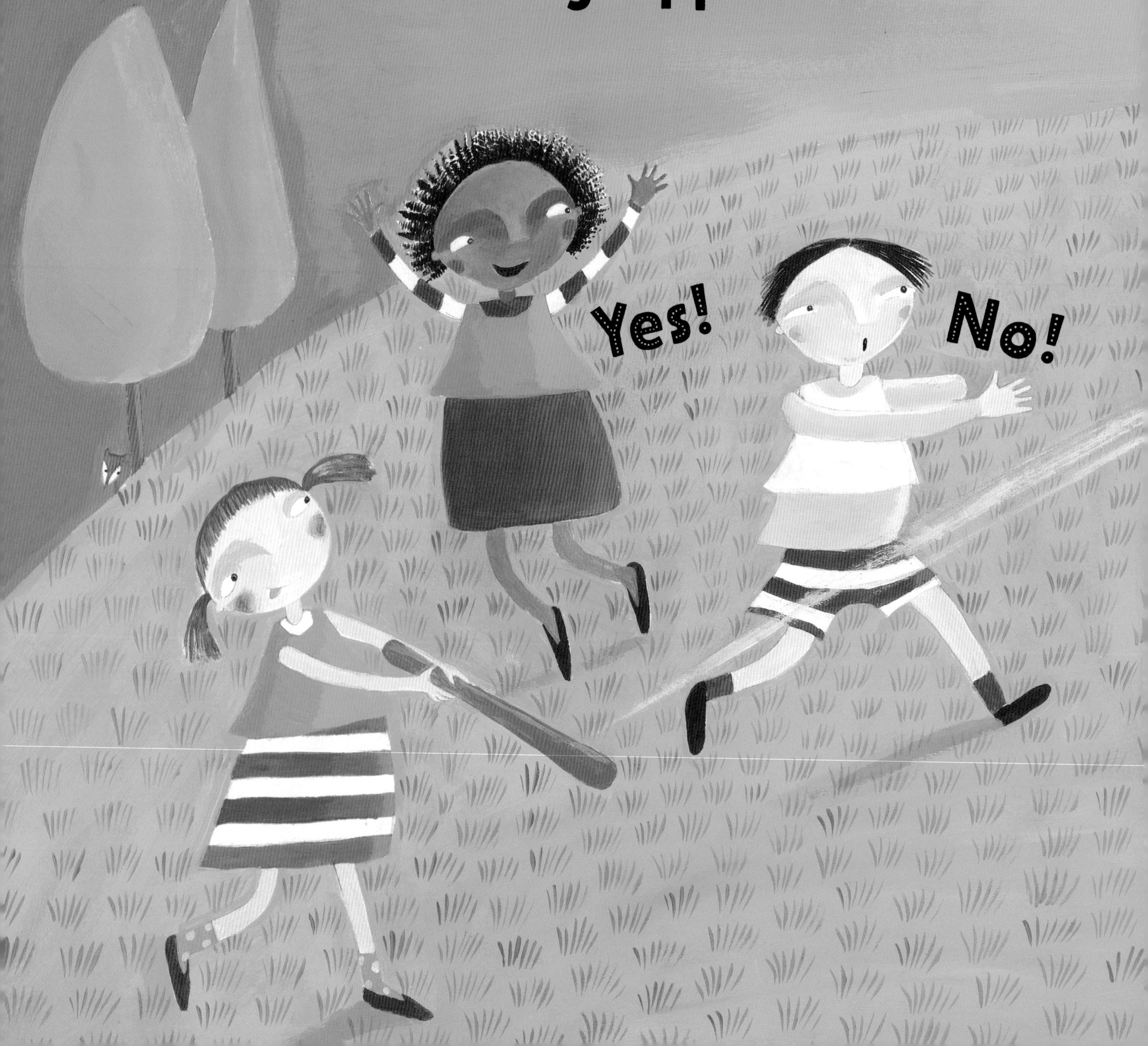

I am doing opposites.

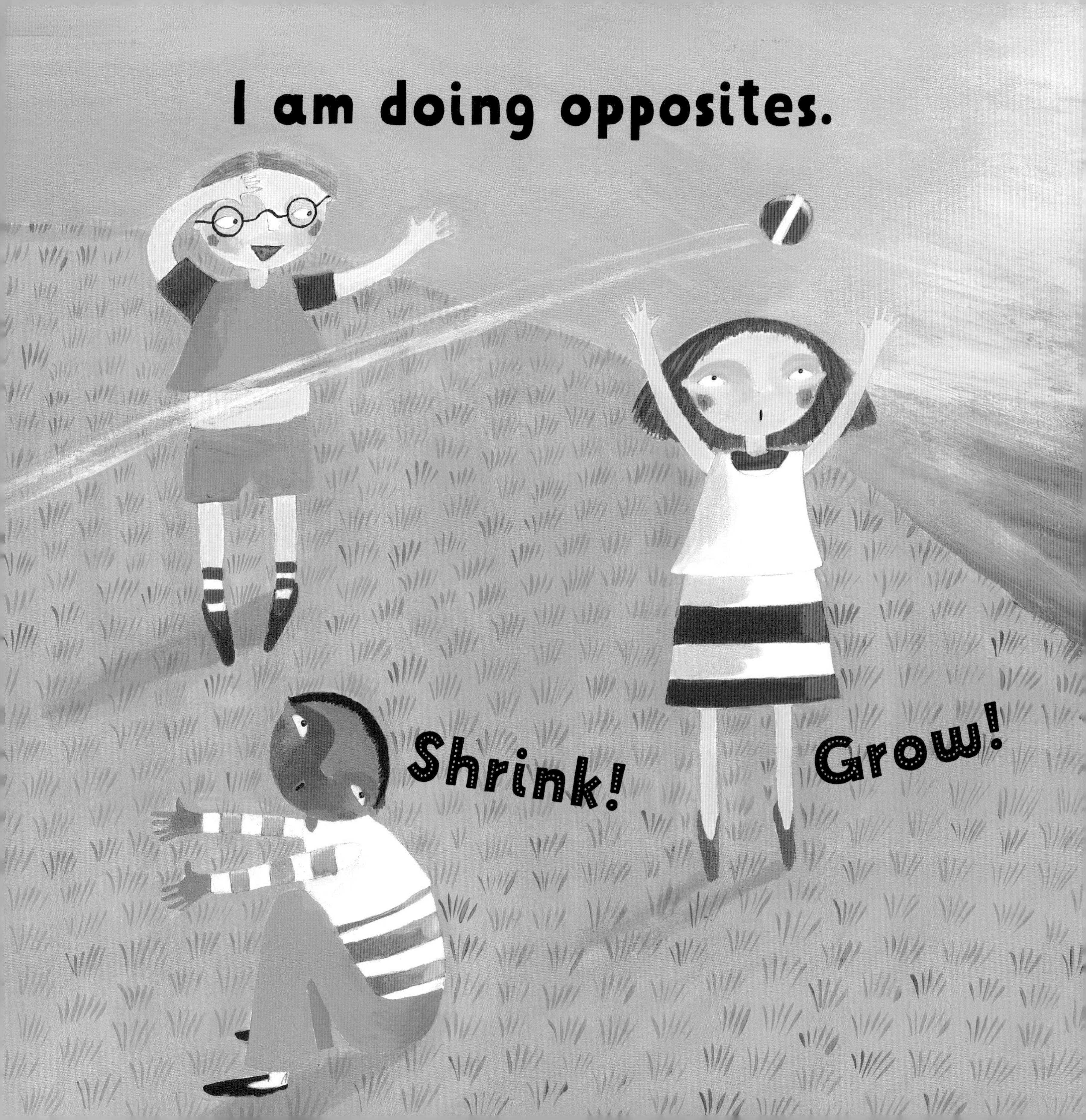

# I can do
# opposites!

# Outdoor Opposites

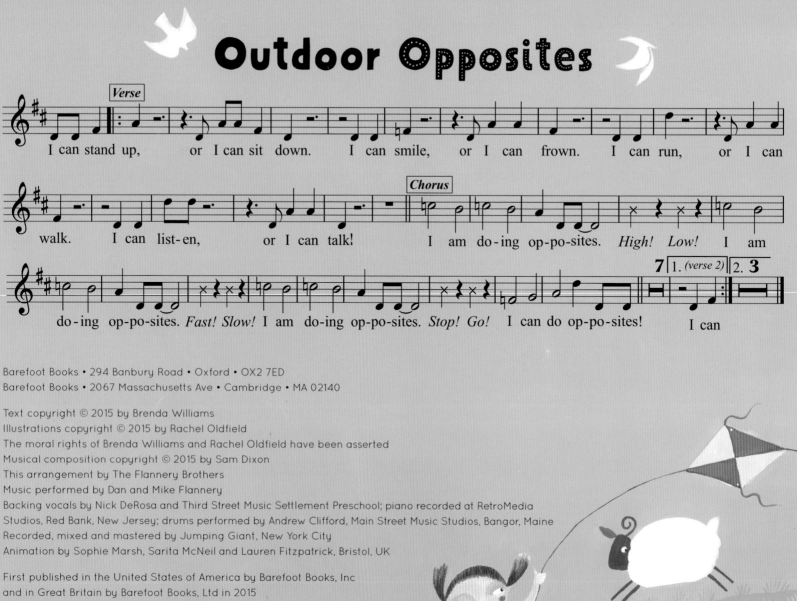

**Verse**
I can stand up, or I can sit down. I can smile, or I can frown. I can run, or I can walk. I can lis-ten, or I can talk!

**Chorus**
I am do-ing op-po-sites. *High! Low!* I am do-ing op-po-sites. *Fast! Slow!* I am do-ing op-po-sites. *Stop! Go!* I can do op-po-sites!

*1. (verse 2)* *2. 3* *7*

I can

Barefoot Books • 294 Banbury Road • Oxford • OX2 7ED
Barefoot Books • 2067 Massachusetts Ave • Cambridge • MA 02140

Text copyright © 2015 by Brenda Williams
Illustrations copyright © 2015 by Rachel Oldfield
The moral rights of Brenda Williams and Rachel Oldfield have been asserted
Musical composition copyright © 2015 by Sam Dixon
This arrangement by The Flannery Brothers
Music performed by Dan and Mike Flannery
Backing vocals by Nick DeRosa and Third Street Music Settlement Preschool; piano recorded at RetroMedia
Studios, Red Bank, New Jersey; drums performed by Andrew Clifford, Main Street Music Studios, Bangor, Maine
Recorded, mixed and mastered by Jumping Giant, New York City
Animation by Sophie Marsh, Sarita McNeil and Lauren Fitzpatrick, Bristol, UK

First published in the United States of America by Barefoot Books, Inc
and in Great Britain by Barefoot Books, Ltd in 2015
The paperback edition with enhanced CD first published in 2015

Graphic design by Katie Jennings Campbell, Asheville, NC, USA
Reproduction by Bright Arts (HK) Ltd, Hong Kong
Printed in China on 100% acid-free paper
This book was typeset in Mr. Anteater, Mr. Lucky, and Mrs. Lollipop
The illustrations were prepared in acrylics

Hardback with enhanced CD ISBN 978-1-78285-094-6
Paperback with enhanced CD ISBN 978-1-78285-095-3

British Cataloguing-in-Publication Data:
a catalogue record for this book is
available from the British Library
Library of Congress Cataloging-in-Publication Data
is available upon request

135798642

# Barefoot Books
### step inside a story

5/15